THE BERRY PATCH

Forgive
and you will be forgiven

Luke 6:37

Judge Not, and ye shall not be judged:
condemn not, and ye shall not be condemned:
Forgive, and shall be forgiven:

Written and Illustrated

by

Denice Goldschmidt

To: Drew Dillainie!
Denice Goldschmidt

1

Many Thanks!

Many people have given me support while producing this book.
My husband, Victor, has been patient, helpful and encouraging beyond measure.
I met bi-weekly with my faithful writing partner, Lisa Feringa, for accountability,
encouragement and prayer. My daughters, Lisa Marion and Leanna, and my prayer
partner of many years, Carolyn Moses, gave hours of editing. And I could not have
done this book without the support of those on my my prayer team. My deepfelt
thanks to each one of you! And thanks to the countless others who supported this
work by being patient as I spent time on it instead of being elsewhere
and doing otherwise.

Finally, I thank the One who called me to this work, my Heavenly Father.
To Him be all the glory!

Text and Illustrations Copyright © 2010 by Denice Goldschmidt
Published by Art Images, P.O. Box 423, Northport, MI 49670-0423
Printed in the U.S.A. by Village Press, Traverse City, MI 49686

Scripture quotations are taken from the Holy Bible, New International Version, Copyright © 1985
by the Zondervan Corporation.

ISBN 13: 978-0-615-36300-4

This one is for

Victor–

my husband, my love, my friend.

I praise the Lord for you and thank you for your desire
to obey and fulfill Ephesians 5:25-26.

Meet the Stufffeds!

Hi! I'm Duffy, a stuffed bear. Do you see me in the sky? I can float because I eat moonbeams. When I'm full, I can carry friends with me.

Snooper is climbing our tree. Like me, he's stuffed. He's covered with patches that hold him together. That's good, because he never sits still.

Annabelle is a rag doll. She's in the top window smiling at you.

Do you see Miss Prissy in the kitchen window? She's a doll, too. She takes care of us kids. We love her - and her cooking!

Now you have met the Stufffeds (*pronounced Stuff-eds*). Come join us in the story that follows and meet one of our woodland neighbors.

4

BERRIES and BRIERS

"I'm going to be the first to fill my pail,"
Annabelle said to herself.

She was climbing her favorite hill to a blackberry patch. "I'm not sure I can beat Snooper, but maybe, just maybe," she said as she quickened her pace.

Every year Duffy, Annabelle and Snooper have a berry picking contest. They each pick from a different berry patch. The first one with a filled pail wins.

"This is no contest," Snooper complains each year. "A contest has a prize!" Snooper usually wins and tells everyone he deserves a prize. Annabelle reminds him the prize is berry pie. "Not fair," he says. "Everyone gets berry pie. I want a *special* prize!"

Annabelle remembered this as she reached her berry patch. "Yum," she said as she dropped handfuls of plump, ripe berries in her pail. Seeing more berries deep in the bushes, she crawled in among the brambles and thorns.

"Ouch - my hair!" she cried. "It's caught!" As she pulled and tugged, knots and tangles tightened.

"Now I'll never win," she sighed. "And my pail was almost full."

Suddenly the branch that caught her began to wiggle. She turned and saw a tiny chipmunk peering down at her.

"Too-tee-too! Too-tee-too," he sang. "What do we have here?"

"I'm caught and can't move," Annabelle groaned. "Can you help me?"

"Hmmm," he pondered. "I can. Yes, I can." His tiny paws moved among the tangles and quickly set her free.

"Thank you!" Annabelle said with relief. "I'm Annabelle," she added. "What's your name?"

"I'm Tudious Foo," he said, hopping to a higher branch.

"Thank you for helping me, Tudious Foo."
She liked saying his name.
"I'd love to invite you to our home
to have blackberry pie with us.
Will you come?"

Tudious Foo swung upside down. He hung by his back paws facing Annabelle.

"No! I will not!" he declared.

Annabelle was taken aback. "But, why?"

"I've seen who else lives at your house - that mean, long-nosed, grungy dog who chases me! No! I will not come!"

Tudious swung right side up and turned his back to Annabelle. "Too-tee-too!" he sang as he skipped through the brambles, his tail held high.

Annabelle crawled from the bushes and straightened her tangled hair. Bothered by Tudious Foo's abrupt answer, she sat at the edge of the hill and stared ahead. Caught under a cloud's dark shadow, she hugged her knees against a sudden chill.

"I'm mad at Snooper," she declared. "I've seen him chasing a chipmunk and I've told him to stop. Now I know it was Tudious Foo. Well, I'm going to do something about it!" She jumped to her feet, grabbed her pail and marched down the hill.

CAUGHT

"Uh, oh," Annabelle said. She stopped marching down the hill and sat in the tall grass. "Something's not right here," she said, her hand on her heart. "I can think of a million words to blast at Snooper, starting with how mean he is! But if I talk to him feeling like this, I might say something I'll regret."

"Hmm. I remember what Miss Prissy always says, '*Pray, Annabelle. Pray!*'"

"Okay," she sighed as she buried her head in her arms.

"Jesus, I'm mad. Snooper's done something awful, but my thoughts aren't good either. Will You forgive me and help me say the right things to him? Thank You."

10

As Annabelle skipped toward home, Snooper dashed out to meet her. "I won! I won! I get the prize!" he yelled, tripping over his paws. "Where have you been? Duffy and I've been back for hours!"

"Hours?" asked Annabelle.

"Well, no. But a long time. Come see my pail! It's really full!"

Annabelle placed her pail beside the others.
Yes, Snooper's was definitely overflowing.
And by the look of his mouth, he had already eaten his share.

"Annabelle, what took you so long?"

"I got caught in the thorns of a berry bush," she said.

"How did you get free?"

"I have a new friend who untangled me."

"A new friend?"

"Yeah - and he knows you, Snooper. His name is Tudious Foo."

"Tudious who?" Snooper scrunched up his nose. "I don't know any Tudious whoever."

"Yes, you do, Snooper. And he knows you very well." Annabelle's face was serious. "He's the chipmunk you chase through the grass all the time."

"Oh, that little guy. I love to chase him. He's fast! The last time I chased him we went around and around until he ducked down a hole. I waited for him to come out and play again, but I got bored and came home."

"Play again? What does that mean?"

"I like to play the chase-game with him."

"Does he ever chase you?" Annabelle asked.

"No! That wouldn't be fun. I'm the big one - the chaser!"

Snooper stretched tall and flexed his muscles.

"I don't think it's play to him," Annabelle said. "I invited him to have blackberry pie with us and he won't come because of you. I think he's scared you'll catch him and hurt him."

"I just want a good race," Snooper said, "and he's great at that! I never thought of catching him, and I would *never* hurt him."

Suddenly, Snooper slid down and sat with a thump. "Uh oh," he groaned.

"Ummm, I remember now. He always - he always yells at me to stop. I thought that was part of the game. I kinda feel awful," he added, pulling his paw to his chest. "What should I do?"

"What do you think you should do, Snooper?"

"I guess I should talk with him. But Annabelle, he might think I'm tricking him. Would you go to him first and see if he'll meet with me?"

"I think your idea is good, Snooper. I'll be happy to."

13

CALLED to FORGIVE

"Tudious Foo! Tudious Foo!" Annabelle called as she followed a path made by tiny chipmunk paws. "Tudious Foo, it's Annabelle. I'm the one you helped untangle in the berry bush. Will you come out? I want to talk with you."

A wiggling nose appeared at the entrance of his home.

"Tudious, I came to talk to you about that grungy dog I live with. He's not here, but he wants to tell you he feels bad about chasing you."

Two tiny eyes blinked in the sunlight.

"He never wanted to scare you, Tudious. He thought you liked being chased."

> "How could he think that?" Tudious said as he pulled back down. "I yelled at him to stop!" he added, his anxious voice muffled by the mud walls. "Why does he do it?"

"For him it was play - like having a fun race."

"I do like to race," Tudious said, his head filling the entrance. "But not with a grungy dog!"

"Snooper - um, Grungy's name is Snooper - Snooper knows he did wrong, and now he wants to make things right with you. I really want you to meet with him."

"No way! I don't trust him."

"I'll come too," Annabelle pleaded. "Snooper wants to ask for your forgiveness."

"Forgiveness? Humph!" Tudious said, slapping his paw on the grass.

14

"Yes, Tudious. To make things right between you, there has to be forgiveness.
Come out. I want to show you something."

Annabelle sat on the soft grass. She patted a spot beside her as Tudious inched toward her.

"Listen to this story Jesus tells," Annabelle said as she opened her pocket Bible. "It's about a king and what his kingdom is like."

Tudious moved closer to Annabelle. His front paws rested on his tummy and his little chipmunk ears stood at attention.

Annabelle turned to Matthew 18:23-35 and began reading the Parable of the Unmerciful Servant.

GOD SPEAKS

"...the kingdom of heaven is like a king who wanted to settle accounts with his servants. As he began the settlement, a man who owed him ten thousand talents was brought to him - **that's like millions of dollars, Tudious.** Since he was not able to pay, the master ordered that he and his wife and his children and all that he had be sold to repay the debt."

"That's awful!" Tudious said, his eyes wide.

"Listen to what happened," Annabelle said.

"The servant fell on his knees before him. 'Be patient with me,' he begged, 'and I will pay back everything.' The servant's master took pity on him, canceled the debt and let him go."

"Wow," Tudious said. "That guy was lucky! Is that the end? I like happy endings!"

"There's more," Annabelle said. "Listen. You'll see what that same servant did."

"But when that servant went out, he found one of his fellow servants who owed him a hundred denarii - that's only a few dollars, Tudious. He grabbed him and began to choke him."

"Ouch!" Tudious shouted, his paw on his throat. "That was mean!"

"'Pay back what you owe me!' he demanded. His fellow servant fell to his knees and begged him, 'Be patient with me, and I will pay you back.' But he refused. Instead, he went off and had the man thrown into prison until he could pay the debt."

"When the other servants saw what had happened, they were greatly distressed and went and told their master everything that had happened."

"Yay!" Tudious yelled. "They told on him!"

"Then the master called the servant in. 'You wicked servant,' he said, 'I canceled all that debt of yours because you begged me to. Shouldn't you have had mercy on your fellow servant just as I had on you?' In anger his master turned him over to the jailers to be tortured, until he should pay back all he owed."

"This is how my heavenly Father will treat each of you unless you forgive your brother from your heart."

Tudious dropped his paws to his sides. He sat still, staring at the ground.

"Um," he said. "Do you think Jesus means that last part - you know, about forgiving from your heart and about torture?"

"I do, Tudious. It's because Jesus knows we suffer inside when we don't forgive."

"But - Snooper's the one who did wrong to *me*!"

"You're right, Tudious. Snooper knows that, and he wants to make things right between you. You have an important part in this - to forgive him when he asks."

"Okay," Tudious sighed. "I guess I'll meet with Grungy - I mean Snooper. I don't want to, but I sure don't want to feel bad inside."

With his head and tail down, Tudious shuffled to his home.

OBEYING GOD'S WORD

"Snooper!" Annabelle called. "Where are you?"

"Here by the shed stacking wood."

"Snooper, I had a good talk with Tudious Foo," Annabelle said as she helped pick up pieces of wood. "He's willing to meet with you. I offered to go too, if that's okay with you."

"Thanks, Annabelle. I guess he doesn't trust me," Snooper said as he tossed a log on the pile. "I don't blame him."

After Annabelle and Snooper finished stacking the wood,
they followed the tiny path to Tudious Foo's home.

"Tudious Foo!" Annabelle called. "Snooper and I are here!"

Up poked a nose and two eyes. *I forgot how big he is*, Tudious thought as shivers rippled down his fur.

"Tudious Foo," Snooper said, trying to speak softly. "I hope you'll forgive me. I only thought of my fun when I chased you. I feel bad about what I did."

Tudious blinked his eyes and looked at Annabelle, then at Snooper.

"And - and I didn't listen when you yelled at me to stop." Snooper hung his head. "I only wanted to play and didn't think of what it was like for you. Will you forgive me?"

Tudious thought about the parable Jesus told and his heart softened.

"I - I think I can," he said.
He glanced at Annabelle.
"Yes, I will. I forgive you."

"And Tudious," Snooper said,
his eyes intent, "I will not chase
you anymore."

"Really?" Tudious asked.
He wanted to believe Snooper.

"Yes," Snooper declared.
"But oh, I do like a good run."

"I like a good run, too!" Tudious
said, stretching his paws in
delight.

"I have an idea!" Annabelle said. "Since you both like to run, let's have a race - a real one between the two of you."

"I'll set it up!" Snooper declared. His ears lifted in excitement.

"No - me! I want to!" Tudious said, stretching on tip-toes.

"Hmmm. I don't think either of you should," Annabelle said.

"Oh, yeah," Snooper said as his ears slid down. "That wouldn't be fair."

"Duffy and I will prepare the track," Annabelle said. "Is tomorrow afternoon okay for the race?"

"I'll be ready!" Snooper said, swiping his paws in the grass.

"Me, tooooo!" Tudious squealed. "See you then," he added as he skipped to his home and slid out of sight.

Snooper pranced beside Annabelle on their way home. "Thanks, Annabelle. You helped me make things right with Tudious. I'm glad he forgave me. And now I have a new friend, too!"

THE RACE

"I'm gonna win! I'm gonna win!" Snooper said to himself as he pranced to the starting line. "I'm gonna beat that little Tudious guy."

Annabelle and Duffy spent the morning preparing the race course. It wound around a meadow marked with flags on the ends of sticks. Tudious and Snooper were shown the route and told the rules.

"I can't get off the track," Tudious reminded himself. "And remember, Snooper, you can't bump into me."

No problem, Snooper thought. *I'll be way ahead anyway.*

Duffy bounced to the starting line. With his flag held high, he made sure Tudious and Snooper were ready. Their paws were on the line. They were bent low. Noses were pointed ahead.

"Ready! Set! Go!" Duffy yelled.
At the swish of the flag, off Snooper and Tudious scrambled.

Annabelle rushed to watch from the finish line. Duffy, full of moonbeams, floated in the air to report what he saw. "They're near the first bend!" he yelled. "Oh, no! They almost ran into each other!"

Duffy lifted higher to see the far side of the field. "It's Tudious by a length! Now Snooper's caught up. They're rounding the last corner. Can you see them?"

"Here they come!" Annabelle shrieked. "They're side by side! It might be a tie!"

"Too-tee-toooo!" Tudious squealed as he flew to the finish line.

Snooper jumped the last stretch, flopped on his tummy and slid to the end.

24

But it was Tudious who finished a chipmunk-nose ahead of Snooper.

"The winner!" Duffy yelled as he float-lifted the paw of Tudious Foo.

Snooper collapsed on his back. "Wow!" he said, gasping for air. "Tudious, you - you aren't even out of breath! How - how come?"

"I'm in good shape, Snooper. Lots of training from a certain new friend of mine!" He flopped beside Snooper as they laughed together.

"Hey! We need a prize," Annabelle said.

"Well...I could share mine," Snooper said. "The blackberry pie I won in the berry picking contest."

"Too-tee-too, tasteeee!" Tudious squealed, rubbing his tummy.

"And I'll even let you have the first bite, Tudious," Snooper said. He swung his front paw in a gracious bow. "Unless - unless a certain someone beats you to the house!"

Snooper sprang ahead, his paws hardly touching the ground. But little Tudious dashed past him in no time.

THE PRIZE

"Yumm," Tudious said as Miss Prissy cut wedges of juicy blackberry pie. "Did you make the pie?"

"She makes it every year for our berry picking contest," Annabelle said, "which isn't really a contest, eh, Snooper?" Annabelle gave Snooper a friendly shove, nearly knocking him over.

"Hey! My pail was the fullest and I got home way before you and Duffy," Snooper said. "But we're both winners, aren't we, Tudious?"

"You are," Miss Prissy said as she passed each of them a plate.

"And Tudious gets the first bite," Snooper said, sniffing his pie.

"Duffy, you offer thanks this time," Miss Prissy said after dishing the last piece.

"Heavenly Father, thank You for the fun we're having together, and for this pie we can't wait to eat! Oh - and 'cuz You reminded us about forgiving each other, we have our new friend, Tudious Foo. Thanks! Amen."

"Hurry - hurry, Tudious," Snooper said, his tongue ready to lick. "Take a bite. I can't wait!"

Tudious lifted his laden fork. Then GULP! His first bite of pie disappeared.

"Annabelle," Tudious said between bites, "I'm glad you read that story about forgiveness to me. But I didn't like that first servant. He was really bad."

"That parable shows us how we tend to act like that servant," Miss Prissy said. "The king is a picture of God. Just like that servant, we do things God doesn't like."

"Yeah," Snooper said, hanging his head. "Like what I did to you, Tudious." Then Snooper's head popped up. "But you forgave me!"

"That's what God does," Miss Prissy explained. "God forgives us because He loves us."

"And we have an important part." Tudious stretched tall to announce what he had learned.

"Because God forgives us, we're to forgive others when they do things to us!"

"That's a good reminder for all of us," Annabelle said as they cleared the table.

"Hey, Tudious," Snooper said after drying the last plate. "Let's go find a place to run!"

"Yeah!" Tudious said.

As they dashed to the door, Tudious darted in front of Snooper, causing him to tumble. "Whoa! Yikes!" Snooper yelped, flying in a ball of fur.

"Oh! I'm sorry!" Tudious exclaimed.

"It's okay, Tudious," Snooper said, hopping to his paws.

"I forgive you!"

THERE'S MORE!

"Miss Prissy! Miss Prissy!" yelled Tudious as he hopped on the picnic bench. He grabbed a berry from the ones Miss Prissy was sorting. "Oh! Is that okay?"

"You may have all the berries you want, Tudious."

"I don't get it," Tudious said. "Annabelle, Duffy and Snooper said I'm a sinner and that Jesus came and died on the cross to take the punishment for my sin. I told them I don't understand it. That's when they said I should come see you."

"All you've said is true, Tudious. When we do things that don't please God, it's called sin. Sin makes God sad because it separates us from Him."

"But you said God loves us," Tudious said. "If I'm separated from Him because I sin, how can I get close to Him?"

"That's why Jesus came, Tudious. Jesus, the Son of God, died on the cross to pay for our sin. He made it so we aren't separated from Him and can live with Him forever. He wants to come and live in your heart and help you live free from the power of sin."

"But how, Miss Prissy? Where is He?" Tudious looked all around.

"This is the exciting part," Miss Prissy said as she set her berries aside and wiped her hands on a towel. "By God's power, Jesus rose from the dead. Later He went to live in Heaven, but He really didn't leave us. He sent His Holy Spirit to live in us. It's like having Jesus living right inside your heart."

"Oh," Tudious said, his eyes wide. "How can I get Him inside me? Will He stay there and help me do what's right?"

"Yes, He will," Miss Prissy said. "If you are sincere and really mean it, you can pray this prayer with me and Jesus will come live inside you."

"Oh, I want that!" Tudious said, clasping his paws. As he bowed his head, Tudious repeated the following prayer Miss Prissy said:

"Heavenly Father, I ask You to forgive my sins. I say with my mouth and believe in my heart that Jesus is Lord and that He died on the cross so I can have life with You in Heaven forever. I believe Jesus rose from the dead. I ask You to come into my life right now and be my Lord and Savior. I will obey You and Your Word in the Bible. You alone are worthy of my praise. Amen."

Tudious lifted his head. "Too-tee-too," he sighed as he pressed his paws to his heart. "He's inside me and I'm free, aren't I, Miss Prissy?"

"Yes, you are, Tudious."

"I can't wait to tell Annabelle, Duffy and Snooper!" he exclaimed. He grabbed another berry and hopped to the ground.

"Too-tee-too!" he squealed as he raced away, tail held high. "I have Jesus in my heart! Too-tee-toooo!"

"Too-tee-too, indeed," Miss Prissy said.

The End

"Will you help me turn this page?"

To the Reader!

If you would like to do what I did and receive Jesus as your Lord and Savior, you can pray the prayer I prayed with Miss Prissy. Talk with one of your parents or an adult that loves Jesus, and ask them to pray it with you. The Stufffeds and I read and study God's Word in the Bible and learn how He wants us to live. You can do that too! It's fun!

Too-tee-too,

Tudious Foo